HOTEL TRANSYLVANIA 2

DRAC IS BACK!

Adapted by Lauren Forte

Illustrated by Joey Chou

Simon Spotlight

New York London Toronto Sydney New Delhi

SIMON SPOTLIGHT

An imprint of Simon & Schuster Children's Publishing Division

1230 Avenue of the Americas, New York, New York 10020

This Simon Spotlight paperback edition August 2015

TM & © 2015 Sony Pictures Animation Inc. All Rights Reserved.

All rights reserved, including the right of reproduction in whole or in part in any form.

SIMON SPOTLIGHT and colophon are registered trademarks of Simon & Schuster, Inc.

For information about special discounts for bulk purchases, please contact Simon & Schuster

Special Sales at 1-866-506-1949 or business@simonandschuster.com.

Manufactured in the United States of America 1015 LAK

10 9 8 7 6 5 4 3

ISBN 978-1-4814-4811-6

ISBN 978-1-4814-4812-3 (eBook)

Count Dracula, owner of the stately and spooky Hotel Transylvania,
loved his daughter, Mavis, more than anything. He loved her so much
that when she fell in love with a human, Johnny, he opened up Hotel
Transylvania to humans so Johnny and Mavis could be together.
—But when Mavis and Johnny got married and had a baby, Dracula
not-so-secretly hoped that his grandson, Dennis, would be a vampire—
not a human.

"Look at all that red hair!" Grandpa Mike said at Dennis's first birthday party.

"It's not going to stay that way." Drac insisted. "I see some black roots on my little Denisovich."

"His name is Dennis, Drac." said Grandpa Mike.

"He likes when I use his vampire name." Drac replied.

"How do you know he's a vampire?" Grandma Linda asked. "He isn't pasty-skinned and doesn't have fangs like you guys do."

"Oh, he'll get his fangs. These things can take some time—up to five years," Drac said.

But as his fifth birthday approached, Dennis still didn't show any signs of being a vampire.

"Ready for our bat lesson, Denisovich?" Drac asked him one evening.

Dennis ran around the room with his arms out and yelled, "I'm a bat!"

"Keep focusing, my little beezlebuddy! You'll be able to turn into a bat eventually!" Drac said hopefully.

"Dad, haven't you noticed that Dennis is different?" Mavis asked. "His idea of scary is Kakie the Cake Monster. And he likes lullabies about twinkling stars, not about pain or blood."

"Sweetheart, if he's going to be around stuff like this, he'll have to get used to it." Drac said.

"Actually," Mavis said, "Johnny and I have been talking about moving."

"What?!" Drac cried.

"Dennis needs to be somewhere safer if he's human," she said. "I'm sorry, but you just can't make somebody into something they're not."

Drac cornered Johnny. "You're in on this? The leaving?"

"It's not definitized!" Johnny answered. "And I don't want to leave. I love it here!"

"Tell that to Mavis!" Drac shouted.

"I did, but all she talks about is going to my hometown to see if it's a good place for Dennis to live." Johnny started to cry.

Drac and Johnny came up with a plan. Johnny would take Mavis to his parents' town, and Drac and the boys would sneak Dennis away to all their old haunts and teach him to be a monster.

As soon as Mavis and Johnny left, Drac packed everyone into his hearse and they hit the road too.

"Where are we going, Papa?" Dennis asked.

"Oh, Denisovich! We're going to have an adventure! A monstery adventure!"

"Monsters like Kakie?" Dennis replied.

"Hey, you know who could fix the kid in snap? Vlad," said Frank.

Drac huffed. "We don't need to call him. We got this."

A short while later they reached the Dark Forest of Slobozia.

"Remember how we used to prowl around and scare the pants off anyone who came into the forest?" Drac asked. "Let's show Denisovich how it's done!"

Frankenstein got ready to jump out at some unsuspecting joggers. But before he could swoop in—

"Hey, it's Frankenstein!" one jogger said, smiling. "Can I take a picture with you?"

"A little selfie action? Sure," Frank answered.

"Really?" Drac asked disappointedly.

Their next stop was Camp Winnepacaca, the vampire camp Drac went to as a kid.

"Denisovich, this is where I learned to catch mice and shape-shift—all kinds of monster stuff," he explained.

"Ooh, badminton!" Dennis yelled.

"That wasn't here when *I* was at camp," Drac said.

"We are so excited to have you visit, Count," said Dana, the camp director.

"I'm interested in sending my grandboy here," Drac told him.

"This little red-headed non-fanger? You sure?" he asked.

"He's just a late fanger," Drac assured him. "That's why we came here. Now, can you show us where you catch mice?"

"Oh, we call it tee-mousing now," Dana explained.

"Why can't we just call Vlad?" Wayne the Werewolf asked.

"Vlad's way always works," said Murray the Mummy.

"I don't want to hear any more about Vlad!" Drac yelled.

When the campers began singing happy songs around the campfire, Dracula had had it. He picked up Dennis and climbed the tower where he'd learned to fly.

"I want to fly like Papa," Dennis said excitedly.

The rest of the monsters followed them.

"Maybe the kid isn't supposed to fly," Frank said to Drac.

"You throw them, and they figure it out. It's how I learned," Drac said defensively. And with that, he tossed a smiling Dennis off the tower. "Papa's right here if you need him!"

"Wheeeeeeee!" Dennis yelled as he fell.

"He's not flying," Frank said anxiously.

"He will," Drac answered calmly.

"Still not," said Wayne.

"It'll happen," said Drac.

"He's getting too close to the ground!" cried Murray.

They were right. Drac soared down and grabbed Dennis before he could get hurt.

"I didn't fly," Dennis said sadly.

"You're trying, my boy," Drac said.

Little did Drac know that a young vampire camper had filmed the whole incident—and the video had gone viral.

As soon as Mavis saw it, she called Drac. "I'm coming home right away!"

Drac and the gang knew they had to get back to the hotel fast.

When they got there, Mavis was waiting for them.

"I was worried Dennis wasn't safe around all the monsters here," she said. "And now I wonder if he's even safe around you. We are definitely moving. Right after his fifth birthday party."

Drac was crushed.

"It's time to see Vlad," Frank said.

"I can't believe I'm doing this," Drac whispered as he entered a dark cave and approached Vlad and his sidekick, Bela.

"Hi, Dad," Drac said, looking down at his feet. "I need your help. My grandson is turning five in a couple of days and he doesn't have his fangs yet."

"We will do it my way—scare the fangs out of him!" Vlad replied.

"So my dad will terrify him until the vampire is scared out of him." Drac explained to Johnny back at the hotel.

"That sounds so harsh." Johnny said. "But it'll be worth it if it means we get to stay."

"Oh, and one more thing: Don't mention to Vlad that you're human—" Drac warned.

"But, Drac, we're all so proud of how we mix so well—" Johnny interrupted.

"Or he'll eat you." Drac finished.

On the day of Dennis's birthday party, Dracula made sure all the human guests were dressed like monsters to trick Vlad.

Mavis hired Kakie the Cake Monster to entertain the kids. Just as he began his show, Vlad, Bela, and their cronies arrived.

Before anyone could react, Vlad levitated Kakie high into the air.

"Denisovich, this is scary. Are you feeling any different?" Drac asked.

"I'm scared, Papa," Dennis said. "What's happening to Kakie?"

Drac saw how horrified Dennis looked. He knew he couldn't let Vlad go through with the plan.

"Stop it!" Drac shouted. "It's not worth it!"

Vlad dropped Kakie to the ground, annoyed.

Mavis was furious with her dad. "This is how you planned to make him a vampire? By scaring it out of him?"

"You're ashamed of The boy because he's human," Vlad said To Dracula.

"There's no shame. I love him no matter what," Drac said. "Everyone here is my family, monsters *and* humans!"

Vlad looked around and realized how many of the monsters there were really humans in costume.

"I can't believe you let your daughter marry a human!" Vlad shouted. "You've betrayed everything we stand for."

"Everything *you* stand for!" said Drac. "We don't hate humans anymore, and they don't hate us!"

"Hey, where's Dennis?" Johnny asked.

In the midst of all the shouting, no one had noticed that Dennis and Wayne's daughter, Winnie, had run off into the woods . . . and Bela had followed them.

"Where could he be?" Drac said, panicking.

"Don't worry. We'll find him," answered Vlad. They set off together to search for Dennis.

Bela found Dennis and Winnie at the dog fort and tried to kidnap Dennis. "You'll be my ransom when I go to destroy that human-loving hotel," he said.

"You can't!" cried Dennis. "It would make Papa Drac sad."

"And what are you going to do about it?" Bela asked, sneering. "You're just a weak little boy."

Winnie bit Bela's hand, and the vampire pushed her away. Dennis faced Bela, his eyes turning fiercely red. He growled and made a vampire face—and bared his fangs! Then he roared so loudly that Bela went hurtling through the air.

Mavis, Johnny, and Drac all heard the roar and flew off toward Dennis. They arrived just in time to see Dennis punch a boulder and shatter it. With the help of all the monsters and humans, Dennis used his new powers to fight off Bela's cronies until they all flew away.

"Dad, I'm so sorry. Dennis is like us," Mavis said to Drac.

"I'm sorry too," Drac replied. "We all just needed to let Dennis find out for himself who he was, instead of trying to tell him."

Even Vlad seemed like a changed vampire.

"Don't ever come near me or my family again!" he told Bela before shrinking him down to a tiny size.

"Hey, isn't it still someone's birthday?" Johnny asked. Together, the monsters and humans sang to Dennis—and celebrated his new fangs!